The Magic Carpet

A SIENA BOOK

Siena is an imprint of Parragon Books

Published by Parragon Book Service Ltd.
Units 13-17, Avonbridge Trading Estate,
Atlantic Road, Avonmouth, Bristol BS11 9QD

Produced by The Templar Company plc, Pippbrook Mill,
London Road, Dorking, Surrey RH4 1JE

Copyright © 1996 Parragon Book Service Limited

Designed by Mark Kingsley-Monks

Printed and bound in Italy

ISBN 0-75251-286-2

The Magic Carpet

Illustrated by Carole Sharpe
Retold by Stephanie Laslett

S
SIENA

There was once a Sultan of the Indies who had three sons, Houssain, Ali and Ahmed. Each Prince was in love with the Sultan's niece, the Princess Nouronnihar and one day the Sultan called them all before him.

"You must each travel the world," declared the Sultan, "and whoever brings back the most unusual gift for me shall win the hand of the Princess."

Many months later the Princes returned. Houssain had a flying carpet, Ali held a magic telescope and Ahmed had an apple.

"This is a magic flying carpet," explained Houssain.

"My telescope will show whatever you wish to see," said Ali.

"My magic apple will cure any sickness," added Ahmed.

The Sultan could not decide which gift was best of all and so he set another challenge.

"Whoever shoots their arrow the farthest shall marry the Princess," he announced. Prince Houssain's arrow went far, Ali's arrow went further and Ahmed's arrow went so far it was lost!

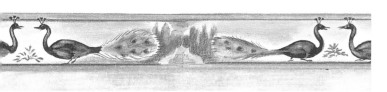

But a beautiful fairy called Paribanou saw where it landed and when Ahmed came looking she went to meet him.

Soon he had forgotten all about the arrow and Nouronnihar. He fell in love with Fairy Paribanou and before long they were married.

Now Paribanou was
very wealthy and when
Ahmed returned home,
the Sultan begged to know
where he had found such rich
clothes and fine horses.
Ahmed would not say, so
the Sultan sent a witch to
follow him.

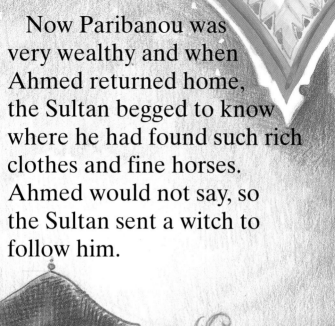

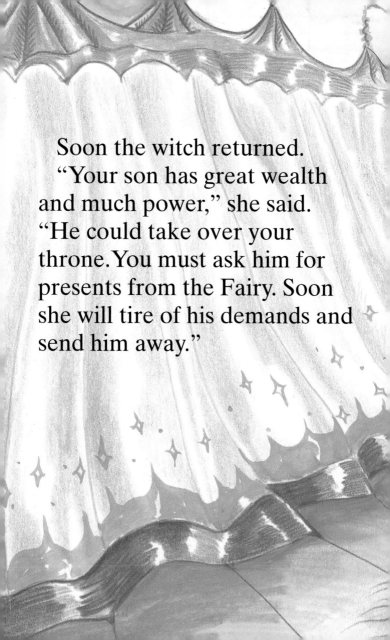

Soon the witch returned.

"Your son has great wealth and much power," she said. "He could take over your throne. You must ask him for presents from the Fairy. Soon she will tire of his demands and send him away."

So the Sultan asked his son for many fine gifts and each time Ahmed was helped by the Fairy.

One day his father asked for a little man with a long black beard. Paribanou laughed.

"That is my brother! I will fetch him for you." she said.

But the little man was very
ferocious and before Ahmed
could stop him he had slayed the
Sultan and half his Ministers.

Then the people decided that
Ahmed and Paribanou should be
their new rulers and so they were
crowned Sultan and Sultaness of
all the Indies.

Prince Ali married Princess Nouronnihar and together they ruled a large province close by, and Prince Houssain decided to spend the rest of his days exploring the world. And the magic carpet? Why, nobody knows what became of that!

Titles in this series include:

Alice in Wonderland
The Wizard of Oz
The Golden Goose
The Happy Prince
The Hare and the Tortoise
The Little Matchgirl
A Little Princess
The Magic Carpet
Peter and the Wolf
Peter Pan
Pinocchio
The Princess and the Pea
Rapunzel
Rumplestiltskin
The Secret Garden
Tom Thumb
The Pied Piper of Hamelin
The Town Mouse and the Country Mouse
Brer Rabbit and the Bramble Patch
Brer Rabbit: Fishing for the Moon